Junior Superstars

Story by Carmel Reilly

Illustrations by Pat Reynolds

Contents

Rigby

HOUGHTON MIFFLIN HARCOURT
Supplemental Publishers

www.Rigby.com
800-531-5015

Chapter 1

Go, Eddie!

Eddie bounced the ball down the court.
He raced past one player and then past another.

"Go, Eddie!" yelled Nina.

Soon Eddie was at the end of the court.
He threw the ball to Nina
and she passed it back to him.
He aimed at the basket. It was a difficult shot.
The ball slid around the top of the hoop
and fell through.

There were shouts and cheers from the sideline.
Eddie's team had won!

Nina and Eddie returned to their classroom.

"I love playing basketball," said Eddie.
"I wish that I could play it all day."

Nina laughed. "You are a great player, Eddie,"
she said.

"You're good, too," he said.

"But I'm not nearly as good as you are," said Nina,
shaking her head.

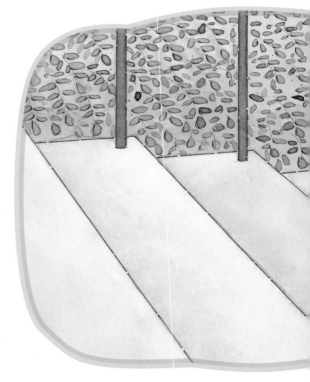

Chapter 2

The Visitor

Mrs. Jacobs, the principal,
came into the classroom with a visitor.
"Hello, everybody," she said.
"I'd like to introduce you to Brad Hill.
He is the captain
of the City Superstars basketball team."

"Brad Hill is fantastic!" Eddie whispered to Nina.
"He's my favorite player. I can't believe he's here!"

"Brad is starting a Junior Superstars team,"
said Mrs. Jacobs.
"He is looking for third and fourth grade players."

"Wow!" said Eddie excitedly.
"I'd love to be on that team."

Brad Hill looked around the room and smiled. "I would like three players from your school to be on the team," he said.

"The teachers will choose our top ten players," Mrs. Jacobs explained. "Their names will be put on the gym bulletin board at lunchtime today."

"I'm going to work with this group tomorrow so that I can select the three best players to be on the Junior Superstars," said Brad.

The lunch bell rang,
and the children quickly put away their books.
"I feel so nervous," said Eddie
as he and Nina raced to the gym.

There was already a big group of children standing
at the bulletin board.
"Yahoo!" one of the girls yelled.
"My name is on the list."

Eddie squeezed in between two taller boys.
"Nina! You're in Brad's group, too!" he shouted.
"And so am I!"

Chapter 3

In the Gym

The next morning, Eddie and Nina
and the other eight children arrived at school early.
Brad was already waiting for them in the gym.

"I'd like to begin with some basic passing, catching,
and defending," he said as they gathered around him.
"First I'll demonstrate some moves
with Eddie and Nina."

Brad tried to pass the ball to Nina,
but Eddie leapt between them and grabbed it.

"Nina, you'll need to keep your eye on Eddie,"
said Brad, laughing. "He's very fast."

Brad threw the ball to Nina again.
She moved quickly behind Eddie and snatched it.

Brad nodded. "That's much better," he said.
"Now the rest of you can work on those moves,
and then we'll try something more difficult."

Later, Brad took half of the children
to the end of the court to practice shooting baskets.

Brad threw the ball to Eddie, who caught it,
took aim at the basket, but missed.

Eddie tried again, but the ball spun
around the edge of the hoop
before it fell back toward him.
Eddie was very disappointed with himself.

The children worked hard
for several minutes.

"You five take a break now," Brad said,
"while I work with the others."

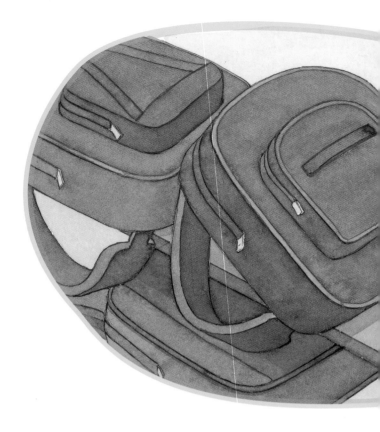

"I was awful," said Eddie, groaning.
"I can't believe that I'm playing so badly today."

"Look at Harry. He's made five baskets already,"
said Nina. "And Lucy is really fast."

"Everyone is so good.
They're much better than me," said Eddie with a sigh.
"I don't think I'm going to make this team."

Chapter 4

Brad Chooses

After school, Nina, Eddie, and the other children
returned to the gym.
Brad Hill was going to meet them there
and tell them who was on the team.

"I really want to be on the team,"
Eddie said to Nina,
"but I played so badly this morning,
I'm sure I won't make it."

"It's me who won't make the team," said Nina.
"But I know you'll be all right."

Brad and Mrs. Jacobs arrived.

"First of all," said Brad,
"I have to say that you were all magnificent
and it was very hard to choose three players.
From fourth grade, I have chosen Harry and Lucy."

"Yes!" shouted Harry, giving Lucy,
who was sitting nearby, a high five.

"And from third grade," said Brad,
"I have chosen Eddie."

Eddie leapt into the air with excitement.
"I can't wait for the first game!" he shouted.

"Oh, Eddie!" said Nina.
"I knew you'd make the team.
I'm going to come along and cheer for you!"